Steve

the

Christmas Ghost

By Craig Hensle

For Karen

1

Christmas Eve

Is there a better day in the year? Christmas seems to come and go in a flash of sticky buns, torn wrapping paper, and howls of delight. After an hour or so of pleasure there is the long wait till the next Christmas. On Christmas Eve the tree is up and decorated. Presents begin to appear beneath the tree. There are parties and visits from relatives bearing gifts. Most of all there is the anticipation of a season, perhaps a whole year. And, still, Christmas lies ahead of us, the hope of a better day yet to come.

But this Christmas Eve was different. An ice storm had rolled in. The parties had been cancelled. The relatives had to stay home. We lost our power early in the afternoon. The house was getting cold. We had all bundled up. I had started a fire. Having a gas stove Erin had started baking hoping the oven might keep the house warm. Baking Christmas cookies by candlelight had kept Tom and Alice busy.

The tree was up and all decorated. It just did not seem the same without the lights on. After baking cookies Tom and Alice had played with their flashlights making patterns on the tree. They had soon tired of that and had gone off to make up their own game.

I was sitting on the sofa in front of the fire. I had wrapped all my presents early in the day. Erin had kicked me out of the kitchen. She said that it was hard enough to cook without electricity. I was just in the way. In the background I could hear the squeal of delight from Alice as her big brother chased her with his flashlight. It might be easy to be upset with Tom for tormenting his sister if you did not realize how much he loved her and how protective he was of her. Alice loved her big brother, too, and delighted in every bit of attention he gave her.

I was staring into the fire when Tom and Alice appeared. They held their flashlights under their chins. "We want a ghost story," Alice said.

"A ghost story, why would you want a ghost story on Christmas Eve?" I asked.

Alice answered, "One of the songs on the radio said there would be Christmas ghost stories and Tommy said there was an evil ghost that took the presents away from bad children and because I was bad the ghost was going to take away all my presents."

I looked at Tom. "Tom, did you tell your sister that?"

Tom pointed his flashlight at the floor and his eyes followed. "Sort of, I guess, I sort of did," he said, " but I didn't think she was dumb enough to actually believe me."

"Are you sorry that you told your sister that?" I asked him.

"Yeah, I guess so," he said, "but she didn't need to go running to Mom."

"What did Mom say?" I asked them.

Alice answered, "Mommy said that if we asked real nice you would tell us a Christmas ghost story. Please. Daddy, please, please, please?"

"Your mother is actually the expert on ghosts. Why don't you ask her for a story?" I told them.

"We did and she said we should ask you," Alice said.

I turned around to look toward the kitchen. By the candlelight I just caught Erin ducking back into the kitchen. I thought I heard her laugh. I looked at Tom. "How about you? Do you want to hear a ghost story?" I asked him.

"Well, sure, I'd like to hear a ghost story," he said.

"You've got to say 'please,' Tommy," Alice told him.

I looked at Tom. "I know that," Tom said. "I was just getting around to it. Please, Dad, can we hear the story?"

"Now you've got to tell us," Alice said.

I picked up Alice and placed her on my lap. Tom climbed onto the sofa and sat next to me. "Let me see," I started. "I guess I'll tell you the story of Steve the Christmas Ghost. Like all ghost stories it is a little hard to believe, but if you have faith it is not hard to believe at all. Steve's story is a little sad, but, like Christmas, it is filled with hope. Now, where should I begin?"

2

Steve and Alfred the Angel

Steve never learned how to love. He grew up without a brother, without a sister, without a mother or a father. Because Steve had no one to teach him about giving he thought life was all about getting.

I don't think we should be too hard on Steve. Without a mother or father he was shuttled from house to house and that was the problem. They were all houses, never a home. As Steve grew up he saw other children so much happier than he was. Steve saw the cars their parents drove. He saw the clothes they wore. But most of all he saw the houses they lived in. Steve thought, "If only I could live in one of those big houses I would be happy."

When Steve grew up he was very good at getting things. Steve did not care how he got things so he did a lot of bad things to get what he wanted. Finally, Steve was able to buy the house of his dreams. The house was a beautiful old home on the crest of a hill overlooking the town. Unfortunately, Steve never got to enjoy this house. A few days after he moved in he, well, he had to visit Heaven.

Steve went to the gates of Heaven where he met an angel called Alfred who was sitting on a very tall chair behind a very tall desk and on the desk was a great big book. When Alfred saw Steve he called out, "Steve, what are you doing here?"

Steve told him, "I want to get into heaven."

Alfred shook his head. "Steve," he said, "you know we can't let someone like you into Heaven. You have done too many things that were not nice. I am afraid you are going to the other place."

Steve was very upset. "It's not fair," he said. "I was too young. I wasn't given a chance to live my life. I would have become a good person. I know it. I'm not going to…."

Alfred stopped Steve from saying anything more. "Don't say it, Steve," Alfred said. "We never say the name of the other place here in Heaven. I am sorry, Steve. I am sorry anytime I have to refuse entry into Heaven and send someone to the other place, but if you had a conscience you know you would just not fit in here."

Steve argued and argued and Alfred politely listened with the patience of an angel. Finally, Alfred held up a hand. "Enough, Steve," he said. "Do you know how to love?"

Steve opened his mouth to say something, but nothing came out. "Just as I thought," said Alfred. "Even you can't claim to love here. It is Heaven after all. You have to understand, Steve. If you don't know how to love you will never be happy in Heaven. You will never be happy anywhere."

Steve had nothing more to say. He turned to go. Alfred went back to studying his book, but when he turned the page Alfred noted something extraordinary. "Stop!" he called out to Steve. "It seems we have more to discuss. Before your mother died she prayed over you. That means you have options."

Steve was elated. "You mean I'm in?" he asked.

Again, Alfred shook his head. "Nothing like that," he said. "But someone who has been prayed over cannot be sent to the other place against their will. You have the option of becoming a ghost and haunting Earth. The rule is that those who are forgotten live on as ghosts. Those who are remembered with love are ghosts no more. It is a rare ghost that makes it back to Heaven. I warn you, Steve. Once the decision is made there is no going back. The life of a ghost is cold and hard. I cannot recommend it. The other place does have a certain warmth about it."

Steve's mind was made up. "I'll become a ghost," he told Alfred. "You'll see. I'm going to get back to Heaven no matter what I have to do. I'll show you." Steve disappeared from the gate to Heaven and went back to haunt his house.

Alfred knew that was not the way to get back to Heaven. He just shook his head and went back to his book.

3

Steve Haunts a House

The problem was that Steve was still Steve. He did not know how to love. He did learn how to haunt, though. Steve was a natural at howling and moaning. His screech has been reported to be one of the most frightening ever. Steve particularly enjoyed appearing out of nowhere with a terrible scowl on his face. Almost as much fun was swooping down on someone unexpectedly. His absolute favorite was chasing someone all around the house, bursting through doors and walls until whoever he was chasing was so scared they ran out of the house to escape. After chasing someone out of the house Steve would retire to the attic full of ghostly satisfaction.

Steve had a lot of opportunities to practice being a ghost. His house was one of the most beautiful in the city. Many people were interested in living in Steve's house. Most of these Steve scared away before they could move in, but a few actually moved in while Steve was not paying attention. That is a problem with ghosts. They are so wrapped up in themselves that sometimes they don't notice what is going on around them.

The people who actually moved into his house did not last long. The longest we know about was two weeks. They were a retired couple. They were thinking of turning the great old house into a bed and breakfast. The first two weeks went by without a peep from Steve. They did not know what all the ghost fuss was about. In a way they were disappointed. The couple had envisioned advertising their bed and breakfast as a uniquely haunting experience. The lack of any ghostly activity was a big disappointment to them, but they thought the house would still make a nice bed and breakfast.

The couple woke up in the middle of the night to a low moaning sound. At first they thought that this was more like it. At last they were hearing from the ghost that they thought they had bought. Then came the howling and the bed started to shake. Next drawers came open and their contents seemed to explode around the room. The howling became loader and they felt something swooping down at them.

Steve had them right where he wanted them. When he thought the time was right he pulled out his favorite trick. He appeared out of thin air inches in front of them with his best, most horrible scowl. The man dove under the covers. The woman ran from the room with Steve in pursuit. He chased her in and out of every room on the second floor, down the stairs, and all around the first floor.

Steve was having a merry time chasing the woman around the dining room table when her husband called out, "Come to the front door and let's get out of here." That is exactly what the woman did. They ran out of house, got in their car, and drove away never to be heard from again.

Steve went back to the attic as close to happy as a ghost can be. Part of Steve, a very little part, did not understand why people were so afraid. Ghosts existed to scare people, but he would never actually hurt someone.

The couple that planned on making the house into a bed and breakfast was the last to buy the house for many years. People were in and out of the house all the time. First there were bank officials. Later there were city officials when the house became city property. Workmen sent by the bank and by the city came to make repairs. When Steve was paying attention he would scare them all until no one would set foot in the house. The only ones who would stay in the house were the spiders who were used to living with ghosts.

Over the years the house fell into a terrible state. The city officials wanted to tear the house down. The house was well over one hundred years old and had been designed by a prominent architect. Also, a prominent family had been the original owners. A group of concerned citizen stopped the city from destroying the old house and was fighting with the city about what to do next when a young couple, an architect and a nurse, fell in love with the old house. The Architect could see the beauty under the unkempt exterior. The Nurse had always dreamed of living in a house as beautiful as this once was.

Everybody told the Nurse and the Architect about the terrible ghost that haunted the old house. The Architect was not sure he wanted to live in a house with a ghost, but the Nurse said, "Oh, come on. We ought to at least check it out. It might be cool."

The Nurse and the Architect checked out the old house. First they walked all around the outside while the Architect noted all the repairs that were needed. Then they went inside and started in the basement. Then they went around the first floor and ended up on the second floor. Everywhere they went they poked in every corner and opened every door. They did not go into the attic. If they had they might have awakened Steve from his sleep and everyone knows a ghost roused from his slumber is particularly grouchy. If Steve had scared the Nurse and the Architect before they moved into the house there might be no story to tell.

When the Nurse and the Architect finished their inspection the Nurse said, "How bad is it?"

"Pretty bad," the Architect said, "but do-able. It will take about two months before we can move in. We will have to do almost all the initial repairs ourselves. No repairmen will work in the house. Maybe after we're living here awhile, but not at first. How about you?"

"Just looking around I can see how beautiful this house must have been," the Nurse said.

"What about the ghost?" the Architect asked. "Do you think he really exists?"

"Oh, he exists," the nurse said. "I can feel him. But he has never hurt anyone so I'm betting he won't hurt us."

The Architect looked skeptical. The thought of living and raising a family in a haunted house seemed to be too much to ask. The Nurse put her arms around him. "I know you're worried," she said. "It is just that I really want to do this and I have a strong feeling that everything will work out."

So, it was decided. The Nurse and the Architect dove right in cleaning and repairing the house. After two months they had enough progress that it was time to move in.

The first night in the house the nurse went right to sleep, but the Architect could not sleep at all. He kept waiting for the ghost to show up. With every creak and groan as the wind whistled around the house he was sure the ghost was about to appear. Nothing happened and after a few sleepless nights the Architect thought, "Maybe this is not going to be a problem. Maybe everyone was just afraid of a spooky, old house." The Architect was finally able to sleep.

The Architect did not know that Steve had been watching the whole time. So much time had passed since Steve scared anybody that he was out of practice. Steve was hoping that if he waited long enough they would just go away. Steve waited and waited. More than a month went by before Steve gave up waiting. He would just have to scare them away. After all, what was a respectable ghost to do?

Just after midnight Steve started in with a low moan. It was the Nurse who noted it first. She shook the Architect awake. "It's happening," she said. "The ghost is finally haunting us. This is so cool."

The Architect was not so sure that being haunted by a ghost was cool. He was also not sure who this woman he married really was. Steve had gone from moaning to an all out, high-pitched wail. The bed was shaking. Drawers were popping open and the contents were flying around the room. Even the walls seemed alive. All the while the Nurse was laughing gaily.

"This is more fun than a roller coaster," she said.

Steve had finally brought out his famous ear splitting shriek. Between the Nurse laughing and Steve shrieking the Architect just covered his head with a pillow and hoped it would all go away.

The racket went on for over an hour. Suddenly, everything became quiet. The bed stopped shaking. There were no socks or shoes or anything else flying around the room. The bedroom, the whole house became very still. The Architect came out from under his pillow. "Do you think it's over?" he said. "Do you think he's gone?"

The Nurse said, "I don't know, but I don't like the quiet."

Steve was preparing for what he hoped would be the shock of the Nurse's life. Just when he thought that the Nurse and the Architect were relaxed he appeared inches in front of them with his most frightening face and with a deafening shriek.

For a few seconds Steve thought he had finally scared the Nurse. She looked surprised. Then she started to laugh again and after awhile she even looked at him and said, "Boo!"

Steve went on shrieking trying to reach new heights in terror, but while Steve was putting all his effort into shrieking the Nurse calmly got out of bed, walked to the door, and opened it.

"At last," thought Steve, "she is trying to escape."

The Nurse, though, turned back to the room. "I thought I would go down to the kitchen and get a glass of milk," she said. "Would you like to come?"

It was Steve's turn to be surprised. He hesitated as the Nurse left the room. "Who does she think she is," thought Steve. "I'll show her who the ghost is."

Steve chased after the Nurse more determined than ever to drive her from the house. Only, the nurse did not cooperate. She would not run. She calmly walked down the stairs, across the foyer, and down the hall to the kitchen. Steve was doing his best to frighten her. He was wailing and moaning and shrieking. He was even making terrible sounds that defy description. Everywhere they went things went flying in all directions leaving behind an awful mess.

At the kitchen door the Nurse opened the door, made a little bow, and motioned as if Steve should go first. "Please, after you," she said.

Steve would have none of it. He waited until the door had closed and then he burst through it. The Nurse did not even see this terrifying display. Her head was in the refrigerator. "Do you like chocolate milk?" Steve heard the Nurse say. "Sometimes if I'm having trouble sleeping I like a glass of chocolate milk."

Steve was furious. Now, a kitchen is no place to have a furious ghost. There are too many pots, pans, and other missiles. There are too many spill-able things. In no time at all Steve created a very big mess. While Steve was creating this mess the Nurse calmly drank her chocolate milk. Oh, every once in awhile something bumped her and Steve did manage to get chocolate syrup on her nightgown, but she never flinched. When she was done with her chocolate milk she rinsed out her glass and placed it in the drain. Before she left the kitchen the Nurse turned back and said in the sweetest possible voice, "Goodnight, Mr. Ghost. Pleasant dreams."

"Why the gall of that woman," thought Steve. "I'm the worst ghost in the whole county, probably the whole state and all the surrounding states." Steve went back to his attic and dreamed just how scared that woman would be on the next night.

The Nurse went back into the bedroom, cleaned up, changed her nightgown, and got into bed with the Architect. "Are you okay?" the Architect asked. "

"I'm fine," the Nurse said. "I told you he wouldn't hurt us. He's just an old softy."

"I should have gone down there with you," the Architect said.

"It's better that you didn't go down there with me," the Nurse said. "This is between him and me. I am not letting him scare me out of this house."

"Do you think it is over?" the Architect asked.

"For tonight," answered the Nurse. "He'll be back tomorrow night. Now hold me. I'm worn out and we have a lot of cleaning up to do in the morning."

The Nurse was right. Steve came back the next night and the next. In fact Steve came back at midnight every night for a month. Then he changed his tactics and every time the Nurse and the Architect fell asleep he would wake them with a terrible shriek. Steve enjoyed that very much, but after trying that for a month the Nurse and the Architect seemed no closer to giving up so Steve took to harassing them all day long. This was very hard on Steve and the results were very disappointing. If the Nurse and Architect were watching TV they would offer Steve some popcorn or ice cream. During the day he would follow the Nurse around creating all sorts of mischief and she acted as if Steve was some sort of puppy. The worst was when the Nurse was preparing dinner and she would ask Steve to get her something or take out the garbage. When nothing happened the Nurse would get a tone in her voice and say, "If you are going to be part of this family you had better start taking some responsibility." That always sent Steve straight to the attic. "I'm a ghost," Steve thought. "I'm not part of a family. I don't have to be responsible. Who does she think she is?"

In the end Steve gave up. He retired to his attic humiliated, a failure as a ghost. He did not know how he could face the other ghosts on Halloween.

The house became still. It was so quiet there was not even a creak or groan when the wind blew.

4

Steve Makes a Friend

Steve was stewing in the attic one day when he heard a noise. A minute later the Nurse climbed up into the attic. "Isn't it enough that she refuses to be scared," he thought. "Now she has to come up here and haunt me, the nerve of that woman."

"Steve!" the Nurse called out.

That got Steve's attention. It had been many years since anybody had called Steve by name. The people Steve had scared had called him many names, but no one had called him 'Steve.'

"That's right," the Nurse said. "I looked you up. I know your name now."

Steve liked hearing his name again after all those years. He was hoping she would say it again.

"Steve," the Nurse said, "I know you're here. I can feel you. Can't you give me a sign that you're listening?"

Steve was sitting on top of an old bookcase. He thought that it wouldn't be too much work to tip over a book.

A book fell out of the top shelf of the bookcase and landed at the Nurse's feet. "Good, Steve," she said, "I came to apologize. I didn't mean to hurt your feelings. I just wanted to live in your beautiful house. Won't you, please, go back to haunting us just a little. Maybe you could give a little wail or moan, but no shrieking. Your shriek is just too powerful. And maybe you could cause something to fly around. I wouldn't even mind if you caused a mess as long as it is not a big mess. Just don't break anything big or important. It might cost too much to replace."

Steve thought about that. It might be more fun to haunt a little, perhaps play a trick or two.

"Good," said the Nurse, "I'm glad we had our little talk. It's just that the house seems so much more alive when you're haunting it. I...."

The Nurse stopped in mid-sentence. She turned around and around. "This is some room you've got for yourself."

The attic was a pretty nice room. There was dust and cobwebs everywhere, but there were windows on all four sides and the ceiling arched up to fifteen feet in the middle so it gave a feeling of spaciousness. The house was surrounded by big trees so that there was not much direct sunlight. Up in the attic you were above the trees that were right next to the house so there was a lot of direct sun. You could also see past the trees for miles. Also, the attic had an assortment of old trunks and boxes and, of course, a couple of bookcases that no one had disturbed for decades. There was, though, no place to sit except on one of the old trunks.

The Nurse walked over to the western window. "Wow! Look at that view," she said. "You can see everything that goes on in town. And you must have great sunsets up here."

Steve had never noticed. Ghosts get so wrapped up in their own problems that they don't really notice the world around them.

The Nurse looked all around the attic one more time. Then she walked over to the hole in the floor that was the entrance to the attic. "You know, Steve," she said, "I love this old house and you are a big part of this house."

When the Nurse had left Steve thought, "Silly woman, a ghost has no use for love."

Steve had not even heard the word 'love' for years. Hearing it seemed to jog his memory. He thought the last time he had heard someone use the word 'love' was that angel he met at the gate to Heaven. No matter how hard he tried he could not remember the angel's name or what he said about love.

That night the Architect and Nurse were in bed. The Nurse had just turned off her light, but the Architect was still reading. Steve began with a low moan and followed it up with a light, almost musical wail. The dirty clothes hamper exploded shooting clothes up to the ceiling.

The Architect was unnerved. He touched his wife. "The ghost's back."

"I know," the Nurse said. "I asked him to do it."

"You what?" said the Architect.

"You'll see," she said. "It won't be too bad. In fact, I find it reassuring. You will too if you turn out the light and hug me."

The Architect wondered what sort of crazy woman would ask a ghost to haunt them. There was nothing he could do about it now and he had to admit that everything seemed better when he hugged his wife. He put down his book and turned out his light. Somehow with the wailing and moaning in the background he drifted peacefully to sleep.

A few days later Steve was sitting on the same bookcase in the attic when he heard a noise. A minute later a bundle popped through the hole in the floor followed by the Nurse. Steve watched as she unwrapped the bundle and started putting together the pieces. When she finished she had a chair that she moved in front of one of the windows where the sun streamed in.

"Oh no!" thought Steve. "She's coming back. The next thing she'll want to do is clean just when I have the dust and the cobwebs almost perfect." Although, he had to admit, you can always use a little more dust.

It was like she could read his mind. "Oh, don't worry," she said, "I'm not going to clean. I know how fussy ghosts are about change. I just want to sit here in the sun for awhile."

The Nurse had started working the nightshift at the hospital. She and the Architect were working different hours. They did not get to see each other as much as she wanted and she was feeling a little lonely. She hadn't planned on anything more than sitting in the sun for a piece. As she sat there she started to talk. She told Steve all about her plans for the future. She told him all about what she and the Architect were going to do to make the house beautiful again. Mostly the Nurse talked about the future of their family. She wanted at least two children, a boy and a girl. The boy's name was going to be Thomas after the Architect's father and the girl was going to be named Alice after her grandmother.

On and on she went holding a very one-sided conversation. Steve thought she would never stop. Eventually the Nurse fell asleep. "At last," he thought, "I finally have some peace and quiet. Doesn't she know that ghosts don't care about that sort of thing?" Then Steve looked over to where she was sleeping in the chair. The sun had moved and she looked cold. He opened one of the trunks, pulled out a blanket, and spread it over her. He even warned away the spiders. All the spiders knew better than to disobey a ghost.

After that when the Nurse was working nightshift she would come home and go up to the attic. She would talk to Steve until she fell asleep. Sometimes they would watch a storm roll in. From the attic they could see lightning for miles. Some days they would watch the birds at the feeders. Steve's favorite thing was to watch a sunset. He had spent all those years in the attic and he had never noticed how beautiful they could be. He even watched sunsets when he was alone, but it just did not seem to be the same.

5

Steve Learns about Christmas

Steve was getting used to having people in his house. While he came down to the bedroom most nights to do a little haunting he still spent every day up in the attic. A time came when a few days passed without the Nurse visiting him. Steve began to wonder if something was wrong. He decided he needed to make sure nothing was wrong.

Steve went to the bedrooms first. In the master bedroom everything seemed in order. The bed was neatly made. There was a fresh coat of paint on the walls. On one wall there was new wallpaper. There were new curtains on the windows that fluttered with the breeze. The other bedrooms had not been touched. They were dirty and dusty with peeling wallpaper and flaking paint.

Steve flew down the stairs. In the foyer there was a new rug and fresh paint. In the family room and the dining room there was new paint, wallpaper, and curtains. Steve found the Nurse and the Architect painting in the kitchen. They were making Steve's house bright and fresh, definitely un-ghostly. Steve felt a twinge of uneasiness thinking about his house being bright and shiny, but when he remembered that was why he had bought the house in the first place the twinge went away. "Perhaps," he thought, "it might not be so bad having people in his house." Steve resolved to pay close attention to all the work the Nurse and the Architect were doing.

The Nurse and the Architect planned on making Steve's house beautiful again. They seemed to be working all the time because there was so much to do. Steve would come down from his attic and float around watching them work until he got tired of watching and returned to his attic.

The Nurse new Steve was watching her and the Architect work. She would have liked to ask Steve to help, but she knew better than to ask a ghost to do that sort of work. Sometimes a ghost likes to make a mess. They just cannot help themselves.

Slowly but surely the Architect and the Nurse put the house back in order. They did most of the work. They painted and papered, laid new floor and new carpet, and hung new curtains. Steve was reminded how proud he had been to own that house. Now he felt lucky to have the house owned by two such fine people.

Steve still had the best ahead of him. It was shortly after Halloween, the only time he got out of the house, when he joined the other ghosts in flying through town, that he noticed the bannister being wrapped with a string of lights. Then he noticed the Architect working on the front of the house with a bunch of tiny lights. The Architect seemed to be wrapping the whole porch with these lights. Ghosts are not too fond of lights. They prefer the dark. Steve knew, he just knew, this could not be any good.

Weeks later Steve was getting lonely one evening up in his attic. He decided to see if anything was going on. When he got to the main floor all the lights were turned on. Steve thought they were beautiful. He looked outside and saw the porch all lit up. Across the street he could see other lights. Steve flew up to the attic and looked out the windows. Everywhere he looked he saw the most marvelous lights. Steve had never seen them before. He had spent all those years so wrapped up in himself that he never noticed these marvelous Christmas lights.

For the first time since he had returned as a ghost Steve wanted to go outside. He wanted to see what his house looked like with all the lights. He wanted to see what all the houses looked like with their lights. He couldn't, though. It was not allowed. Of course, every year just before midnight on Halloween he raced through town with the other ghosts. That was different. He did not really have a choice on Halloween.

Instead, Steve decided to see if there were any other decorations in the house. He found a house filled with decorations. The Nurse and the Architect loved Christmas and wanted to turn their house into a Christmas wonderland. While they decorated almost everywhere and everything, it was the tree that they were most proud of. The family room had an extra-high ceiling so the tree was extra-tall. The Nurse had been collecting ornaments since she was a little girl. For the first Christmas in their new house the Architect had bought all new lights.

The Nurse and the Architect had just spent an entire day buying, putting up, and decorating their Christmas tree. They sat in the dark enjoying the lights twinkling on the tree when Steve found them. Steve thought the tree the most magnificent thing he had ever seen. First, he hovered over the tree. Then he watched the lights twinkle from all four sides. Then Steve repeated the process, but this time he looked at each and every decoration on the tree.

Steve could not get enough of looking at that tree. Steve was very disappointed when the Architect turned out the lights and the Architect and the Nurse went upstairs to bed. Steve had enjoyed the decorations so much that he decided to come down out of his attic every day. He did not want to miss a thing about Christmas.

Steve was floating about in the family room one day when the Architect came home. He closed the front door very carefully. He tiptoed up the stairs. He was carrying a couple of large shopping bags. Steve thought he was acting very suspiciously and decided to follow him. The Architect put the bags on a high shelf in a closet in one of the bedrooms that had not been painted yet. Steve thought this was very unusual behavior. He wondered what was so important in the bags that the Architect had gone to so much trouble.

The next day the Nurse came home, looked all around, and found the Architect working in his den. She closed the door. Then she went outside and returned with several bags that she hid in the attic.

Steve had never seen the Nurse or the Architect act that way before. He decided he would keep a close watch over those bags to see what happened.

A day came when there was a lot of commotion in the house. People came and left behind packages all brightly wrapped in paper with ribbons and bows on them. The packages all ended up under the tree. Later that night both the Nurse and the Architect got out the bags they had hidden away and wrapped the contents in gaily colored paper and put big bows on them. Then they put them all under the tree before going to bed.

Steve made sure he woke up with the sun. He did not want to miss a thing. Hours later the Nurse and the Architect came downstairs. They put on music and turned the lights on the tree. To Steve the Nurse and Architect seemed to take forever before they got down to the business of opening presents. They took turns opening presents. After every present there were kisses and hugs. Steve floated nearby trying to see each and every present. They all seemed so wonderful except for the sweater from Aunt Martha, but the Nurse did not seem to mind so much.

Later that day other people arrived at the house. There were more presents. People were saying, "Merry Christmas!" Everyone ate and drank and had a good time.

Steve had been aware of Christmas growing up, but he had never celebrated Christmas, never given a present, and never received a present. He had never even decorated a tree. Steve thought, "So, this is what Christmas is all about. I think I like it."

Christmas became Steve's favorite thing. When the Architect took down all the lights Steve felt awful and refused to come out of his attic for days until he realized that he could always look forward to next year's Christmas.

Steve did not have long to wait. It is a little known fact that ghosts do not experience time the same way we do. What would be a week for us feels like a couple of days to a ghost.

When Christmas rolled around again Steve was ready. He thought the house more beautiful and the tree bigger and more magnificent than the year before. There seemed to be more of everything. Steve was correct about this. The Nurse and the Architect collected decorations all year long and added what they collected to the ones they already had.

Steve paid close attention to the Nurse and the Architect. Both sneaked presents into the house and hid them away. The night before Christmas both the Nurse and the Architect wrapped their presents and placed them beneath the tree.

When the Nurse and the Architect went to bed Steve was left alone with all the presents. He examined each and every one of the presents. Steve found the presents exciting. They were all so gaily wrapped. He had never received a present so he had never experienced opening a present. He began to wonder what the bright wrapping and colorful ribbons held. He picked up the presents one by one and shook them. That did not tell him a thing. The more he thought about the presents the more he wanted to know what was in them. An idea came to Steve. Maybe he could open a present or two. He would not open the big ones, but maybe he could open a couple of the small ones. Then, once he knew what was inside, he would rewrap the presents. After all how hard could it be?

Steve chose two presents, one with Christmas trees on the outside and one with snowflakes. Steve tried to be very careful unwrapping the presents, but the wrapping paper had so much tape on it the paper tore. At first the smaller one was a disappointment. All it held was a wallet. But after Steve had a chance to examine it he decided it was a good wallet and he would not mind getting a wallet like that himself though he had no idea what a ghost would use it for. The other present contained a bottle of perfume. It had a sprayer and he sprayed it right in his own face. "Ick! Much too flowery," Steve thought. He preferred the smell of dust and mold and mildew. Still, the scent did remind him of the Nurse and, well, she was sort of nice.

Steve tried to rewrap the presents. The wrapping paper had torn too much when he had unwrapped the presents. No matter how Steve tried he could not make them look like they were before he unwrapped them. Steve did the best he could and hid the rewrapped presents under other presents. Steve was sure no one would notice.

On Christmas morning the Architect was hunting around for just the right presents to be the first ones unwrapped. Under a much bigger box he found two presents with the paper torn. One was for him and the other was for the Nurse. He handed the Nurse her present and looked at her for an explanation. The Nurse knew right away. "Steve," she said. Both the Nurse and the Architect laughed.

Steve was so embarrassed that he flew up to his attic. He did not stay there long. He wanted to be downstairs with the Nurse and the Architect. He wanted to see them open every present. He wanted to experience the joy that they felt on Christmas. Steve had learned his lesson. He would never try to unwrap a present again. Every Christmas after that he made sure he knew what the presents were before they were wrapped.

To Steve the next Christmas was even more magnificent. There were more presents and more lights. The whole house seemed to be covered with decorations. The Christmas tree was particularly spectacular, but Steve thought he could make it even better.

On Christmas Eve after the Nurse and Architect went to bed Steve got busy. Some of the ornaments were in the wrong place and the lights were not evenly distributed. In moving everything around he knocked a couple of ornaments off the tree and they broke. "Oh, well," thought Steve, "a little breakage in the pursuit of perfection is expected." He did try to be more careful.

When Steve had finished with the lights and the ornaments he turned his attention to the most important thing, the top of the tree. The last two years there had been a star on the top of the tree. This year there was an angel. Steve definitely approved of the change. He was after all an expert on angels having met one. The problem was that the angel was bent over. That would never do. An angel had to be upright. Steve floated to the top of the tree and tried to straighten the angel. Nothing that he tried seemed to work. Finally, he bent the top of the tree enough that he felt something give. When he let go the angel stayed straight for just a second before it toppled to the floor knocking down ornaments as it fell. "Oh, no," thought Steve, "this would never do." He picked up the angel and put it back on top of the tree. Now the only way the angel would stay on the tree it was tilted worse than before.

Steve decided to leave everything alone. He just could not do anything right. He spent the whole night worrying that he had ruined Christmas.

The next morning he did not want to be in the family room when the Nurse and the Architect came down to open presents. Instead he just stuck his head through the ceiling so he could see what happened.

When the Architect observed the wreckage around the tree. He turned to the Nurse and said, "Steve."

The Nurse just waved it off. "It is still a beautiful tree. I'll clean up the mess later. Let's open some presents."

Steve had not ruined Christmas by ruining the tree. "Maybe," thought Steve, "Christmas is about more than a Christmas tree." Steve thought he knew what Christmas was all about. He still had a lot to learn.

6

Tom

The next year the Architect and the Nurse had a baby boy. They called the boy Tom. Steve was very interested in this baby, but the baby smelled funny as all babies do so Steve stayed away.

The problem was that Steve was lonely. The Nurse was so busy with her new baby that she never came to the attic anymore. She never came to see the storms roll in, or watch the birds fly around, or watch a sunset with him. When Steve saw a particularly beautiful sunset he missed her most of all.

After several months of feeling lonely Steve decided he had to check out this new baby. Steve stuck his head down through the ceiling and looked around. The smell did not seem to be so bad. He liked the color blue on the walls. The baby was in the crib. Tom did not do very much. Steve thought Tom was sleeping. Steve looked around the room. There were piles of toys. Steve decided to float down and test them out. He found a brightly colored ball that made noise when you rolled it and lots of stuffed animals.

Steve heard a sound from the crib. He floated over the crib to get a good look at this boy. Steve was surprised when Tom smiled at him. Could the baby actually see him? Steve moved left, then right. The baby seemed to follow him. That was interesting. No one else could see Steve except when Steve wanted them to see him.

Steve picked up a rattle and shook it. Tom watched the rattle closely as Steve traced a variety of patterns in the air over the crib. Tom even laughed. Steve thought the laugh sounded like music.

Tom got a funny look on his face. After that he started to cry. This was not a sound Steve enjoyed hearing. Steve shook the rattle harder. He made funny faces. Nothing he could think of stopped Tom from crying. When the Nurse started through the door to the nursery Steve dropped the rattle and flew right through the ceiling into the attic. "What did I do?" thought Steve. "Tom and I were having such a good time and then he started to cry." Steve did not know that sometimes a baby cries when they need their mother.

Steve was hooked. Playing with Tom and his toys was the most fun he had in a long time. Steve went to Tom's room as much as he could, but he kept two rules. Steve never woke Tom if Tom was sleeping and Steve always left the room as soon as the Nurse arrived.

Christmas rolled around as it does every year. Steve thought he knew all about Christmas. He was very surprised that the addition of little Tom made everything even better. There were more decorations, new ones meant for a child. There were more presents than before. The Nurse and the Architect seemed happier and more excited.

Christmas Day came and Steve watched the Nurse and the Architect open presents. Tom was too small to understand what was going on, but the Nurse and the Architect acted like Tom could understand everything. While Steve watched this merry scene unfold he noted one set of decorations. It was a nativity scene. Steve saw a mother and a father and a child. Steve had never noticed this before. The more he watched the Nurse, the Architect, and Tom the more he thought about the nativity scene. "A mother, a father, and a new baby," Steve thought, "is this what Christmas is all about?"

As time went by Tom started to crawl and then walk. Tom became even more fun. Tom was interested in everything. That meant there was nothing safe in the house.

One day when Steve was still in his attic the Nurse climbed in. She rarely came to the attic anymore. Every once in awhile she would come to the attic to put something in or get something out of one of the trunks. She never came to talk about her dreams anymore. Or fall asleep in her chair even though she often looked tired. This time the Nurse sat in her chair for a time. At last the Nurse said, "Steve, I want to ask a favor."

Steve thought, "Who does she think she is asking a favor of a ghost?"

"I want you to look after Tom," the Nurse said. "This is such a big house. No one knows the house like you do. There is so much trouble a little boy can get into, especially one as active as Tom. I would like you to watch over him and keep him safe."

"Why the nerve of that woman," thought Steve. "Doesn't she know that ghosts have things to do?" In fact, ghosts do not have things to do. Ghosts have nothing but time. Steve did have to admit that it was a big house and no one knew the house better than he did. Steve even knew all the spiders by name.

The Nurse turned to go. Just as she was leaving the attic the Nurse turned back. "Please, Steve, would you do this for me?" she said. "I would appreciate the help."

It was one thing for a ghost to do what he wanted when no one was looking and quite another to do what people wanted him to do. Steve stayed up in his attic for several days and while there was a particularly beautiful sunset and the birds were playing at the bird feeders he did miss playing with Tom.

"Perhaps I will watch over Tom," thought Steve. So Steve went back to playing with Tom.

Steve may not have been a good influence on Tom. Boys at that age love creating a mess. Of course, boys at that age don't think of it as a mess. They think that is what the world is supposed to look like. The only ones who like messes more than little boys are ghosts. They know they are creating a mess, but do it anyway. Little boys learn not to create a mess when their mother tell them what they did was bad. Ghosts never really learn. The Nurse would discover the mess. She would scold Tom and send him to his room. Then she would scold Steve saying that he should have known better. When this happened Steve would fly up to his attic where he would think, "But I'm a ghost, doesn't she know I can't change?"

After one particularly bad mess Steve stayed in his attic for two days. Steve missed playing with Tom so much that he finally decided to leave his attic. It was a good thing he did. Tom thought he should be able to fly. Tom had seen Steve do it so why couldn't he. Tom was constantly jumping off tables and chairs to see if he could fly. This time Tom was going to jump off the stairs. Worse yet, he was going to take a running start. Steve came out of the attic just in time to see Tom running toward the top of the stairs. Steve rushed down and caught Tom just as he jumped. Steve eased him back down. Nothing serious had happened, but Tom did not know that Steve had saved him. He thought the reason he had floated back to the ground was that he could fly. After that Steve had to keep a close eye on Tom.

One of Tom's favorite things to do was draw with crayons. For some reason Tom was never satisfied with just drawing on paper. He had to draw on walls. One time the Nurse caught Tom drawing on the walls in one of the spare bedrooms. She was quite angry with both Tom and Steve. Steve did not know what the problem was. He thought the crayon drawings were an improvement.

Steve found a way that Tom could draw on walls without any problems. Steve took Tom to one of the bedrooms that had not been decorated yet. The room had been cleaned, but the walls still had the old paint and wallpaper. "Here," Steve thought, "Tom can color all he wants."

No one had asked the Nurse. One day she discovered Tom coloring the walls. Steve could tell by the look on her face that she was very angry. Steve flew up to the attic and poked his head through the ceiling to see what was happening. The Nurse looked at the wall where Tom had been coloring. There was a picture of a bed. Over the bed floated a cloud with arms and legs and a smile. A few feet away there was a picture of a Christmas tree with presents and a short, medium, and tall person.

Tom was already crying. The Nurse bent over and hugged Tom until he stopped crying. Steve heard her say, "Okay, you can color in here, but no place else. Do you understand?" Tom nodded and the Nurse gave him a big hug and kiss.

Tom loved to run. It always amazed Steve that anybody could get such pleasure from running as fast as he could around the house. The problem was that there was a lot that was breakable in the house. With Tom running as fast as he could he would bump into a lot things knocking them over. Steve was left with the task of catching them before they hit the floor and broke. This was counter to everything Steve believed in as a ghost. To a ghost things falling and breaking was simple joy, but he knew that was not what people believed so he minimized the damage as much as he could. Almost nothing of importance broke except for that one time. Tom was playing a game running in a circle around the living room. He had just knocked over a lamp. Steve caught the lamp while seeing Tom disappear into the foyer. Steve was carefully placing the lamp back on a table when he heard a crash. When he got to the foyer he found Tom standing over Grandma's broken vase with flowers everywhere.

Tom was already crying when the Nurse showed up. She looked at the mess, bent over, and hugged Tom. "Tom," she said, "you are becoming a big boy now. We all know how much ghosts like to make a mess, but you have to help Steve so he does not do this again. That vase was my grandmother's special vase. It cannot be replaced. You've got to make sure that Steve is more careful in the future. Can you do that for Mommy?"

Tom gave his mother a big kiss and hug, but poor Steve was upset. Steve had been trying to save everything from breaking and now he gets blamed for breaking Grandma's vase. Steve flew up to his attic and thought he might never come out again. It would serve them both right never to see him again. But after he thought about it for a while he realized the most important thing was that Tom was happy and safe.

Perhaps I should tell you what happened to Tom, Steve, and the toilet, but I think we can save that for another time. Tom was always having adventures and Steve was having more fun than he had ever had before. Tom was just so active and creative that every day was different. Still, the best thing was Christmas. Having a child around had just changed everything about Christmas. Now there were new toys every year. The Nurse, the Architect, and Tom created such a scene of joy that for the first time Steve was happy to be a ghost. And every year there was that same nativity scene with the mother, the father, and a new baby. "Yes," Steve thought, "Christmas is so much better as a family. That must be what Christmas was all about."

As time passed Tom spent more time out of the house. There was something called pre-school that took Tom away. Also, Tom enjoyed playing with friends in the yard of the old house. Steve watched Tom through a window. A few times he went out on the porch. Being outside, even on the porch, made Steve feel very uncomfortable.

Steve realized that Tom was growing up. Steve wondered how long before Tom became like the grownups and could not see Steve except when he put on one of his ferocious faces. When Steve thought about it he saw that everything around him was changing, but he would always be a ghost.

7

Alice

Spring came and brought a new baby girl. The girl's name was Alice. Steve was very excited. Now that Tom had found other friends and spent so much time away from the house Steve was hoping he could be friends with the new baby. When Alice was brought home for the first time Steve watched very carefully for a time when the Nurse left Alice alone. Steve had to wait for days and days. Alice was a newborn and the Nurse was being very careful. At night Alice was laid down to sleep by herself, but all Alice seemed to do at night was sleep and cry until either the Nurse or Architect came for her. Steve decided it would not be a good idea to introduce him self to Alice at night. He might get blamed for making Alice cry. Steve also wondered whether seeing a ghost at night might be too much for a little baby.

Steve waited weeks until he found just the right time to take a close look at little Alice. The Nurse laid Alice down for an afternoon nap and left the room. Steve floated low over the crib and took a good look at Alice. He thought Alice was the prettiest thing he had ever seen. If she would only wake up before the Nurse returned Steve could find out if Alice saw him the same way that Tom did.

Steve floated over the crib waiting for Alice to awake while keeping an eye out for the Nurse. At last Alice woke up. Steve flew in close. Alice seemed to be looking at him, but when he flew to the left and then the right Alice's eyes did not appear to follow. Steve zoomed all around the room and did all sorts of aerial acrobatics. Nothing pulled Alice's attention away from her feet.

Steve flew back to his attic. He was very unhappy. Tom had been able to see Steve without Steve putting on one of his ferocious appearances. Steve and Tom had become special friends. Now Tom was growing up. Pretty soon Tom would have lots of friends. Steve wondered if soon Tom would be like all the other grownups that could only see Steve when he put on a terrible face. Steve knew there was nothing he could do about Tom growing up. Steve even wanted Tom to grow up because he knew that was what was supposed to happen. Steve did have such high hopes for Alice.

Steve went to the window to watch the sun set. A beautiful sunset always made him feel better. That night the sunset was particularly colorful, but Steve barely noticed. Steve stayed in his attic for several days. He did not even venture out in search of Tom. Every once in a while he would stick his head through the ceiling of the nursery to watch Alice. She was such a pretty little thing that just seeing her made him feel better. Steve decided that even if Alice could not see him he could still entertain Alice by bouncing balls and shaking rattles and all sorts of other things. That is what he did and every time Alice smiled his heart would melt, that is, if he had a heart.

Christmas came and went. Steve thought he was an expert on Christmas. He had to have everything just right. The Nurse and the Architect did a pretty good job of decorating the house. Steve did not mind helping them out a bit by making sure every display was just perfect. He would make little adjustments here and there. Of course, Steve had to follow Tom around. Tom wanted to play with every decoration. It was a full time job putting decorations back in their perfect places after Tom had gotten through with them, but when friends and neighbors called and complimented the house Steve knew, he just knew it was his attention to detail that made the difference.

Steve still watched over the wrapping of all the gifts. He even graded all the gifts. The Nurse always seemed to buy the right thing. The Architect was another matter. The Architect did pretty well in buying gifts for Tom, but he never bought good enough presents for the Nurse. At least, that is what Steve thought.

The best part of Christmas was Christmas Day. A new child made it even better. There were more presents and more joy. Steve could not wait to see all the presents opened. He knew what each of them was, but watching someone open their present somehow made it all new again. So, Steve floated in his favorite spot by the nativity scene, where he could see everything going on around the Christmas tree and kept up a running commentary with the mother, father, and baby in the nativity scene as if they were listening to everything that he said.

Time passed and Alice was over a year old. She was starting to take an interest in coloring things. Steve expected Alice to want to color on the walls because that was what Tom did. Alice did not act anything like Tom. When she colored she only colored on paper and it had to be very precise. Steve was watching her color one day when Alice just handed him a crayon. Steve started to color with it. Alice handed him another crayon. Steve stopped. "Does this mean she can see me?' he thought.

Steve decided to fly around the room. Alice watched him wherever he went. As Steve realized that Alice could see him his spirits soared. Steve zoomed around the room flying loop-de-loops and all sorts of crazy patterns until Alice began to laugh.

From then on Steve had the best time playing with Alice. She was not the bundle of energy that Tom was. There were no attempts to fly. Alice did not like to run around, knocking things over the way Tom did. She did not even like making a mess. Alice did like to play games with lots of rules that Steve always seemed to break. Steve did not like breaking the rules, but Alice was always very kind to him. She always wanted to be sure that Steve was getting his fair share. If they were coloring she gave Steve half her crayons. If they were playing tea party she made sure Steve had his own cup and got the first choice of cookies. Whatever they did together Alice was always happy and her laugh made Steve forget he was a ghost.

One day something unusual happened. Alice was napping. Steve was in his attic. The Nurse came up to the attic and sat in her chair the way she used to do. The Nurse was quiet and Steve just watched. It had been years since the Nurse had come to the attic to talk. Every once in awhile she came to get something out of storage. Steve thought she looked sad. After awhile the Nurse said, "Steve, I would like you to do me a favor. I need you to watch over Alice."

The Nurse got up and left. At first Steve was indignant. "Of course I will watch over Alice," he thought. "This is my house. I watch over everything in it even the spiders. No one has to tell me to watch over anyone, especially Alice."

There was something wrong. Steve knew it. He just did not know what was wrong.

Steve marked the passing of the years by Christmas. With Tom and Alice in the house every Christmas was better than the last. There was for Steve one thing wrong. Every year he watched the happiness and joy of the Nurse, the Architect, Tom, and Alice as they opened presents. Steve very much wanted to give a present. He had watched the unwrapping of presents closely every year. It was clear to him that the Nurse and the Architect had the greater joy in giving. It would be nice to receive a present, to know that someone was thinking of you, but giving was clearly better.

It was Christmas just before Alice's fourth birthday. Steve was overseeing the hanging of the stockings as he did every year. The Nurse was helping Alice hang her stocking when Alice just stopped. "What's wrong, honey?" the Nurse said.

"What about Steve?" Alice said.

"What about Steve?" the Nurse said.

"Shouldn't we be putting up a stocking for Steve?" Alice said.

"Maybe we should," said the Nurse., "but what would we put in it? What would a ghost want?"

Steve listened very carefully because even he did not know what a ghost would want. Alice thought for a while. "Steve always likes the pictures I draw," she said. "Maybe I can draw a special Christmas picture for him."

"It was true," thought Steve. "I always enjoy the pictures that Alice makes and a Christmas picture would be special."

"I think that would be good," said the Nurse.

Tom had been listening. "Can I draw a picture, too?" asked Tom.

"I don't see why not," said the Nurse. "I think I have a spare stocking that we can decorate just for Steve."

The next morning was Christmas. Tom and Alice were too excited to notice that Steve's stocking was missing. The Nurse noticed. All she did was smile. A few days later the Nurse went up to the attic to get something out of storage. She found the stocking and over by the window she found the pictures drawn by Tom and Alice. They had both drawn the same thing, a family portrait with a Christmas tree, a mother, a father, a sister, and a brother with a ghost floating over them all.

For Steve getting the pictures made that Christmas the best. He still had not given a present. Steve knew that he had to give a present to know what Christmas was all about. He vowed that he would find a way to give the best Christmas present ever.

8

Steve Visits Alfred

Halloween was always a tough time for Steve. It was the only time he was allowed out of the house, although that does not really describe what happens. On Halloween in the hour just before midnight Steve felt a force pull him outside to race around town with all the other ghosts. At midnight Steve returned to his house. The rest of the time if he left the house he began to feel ill. The further he went from the house and the longer he stayed away the worse he felt. Steve had tried it once when he first returned to haunt his house. After all, rules were not meant for the likes of him. He thought he could do whatever he wanted, but his first experience away from his house convinced him not to try it again.

At first racing around town with all the other ghosts seemed like a good idea. Steve even tried to talk with some of the ghosts, but most just ignored him. Some were downright grouchy. After awhile Steve found Halloween depressing. He saw so many ghosts rising out of cemeteries and coming out of the old houses. Steve felt sorry for all these lost souls. Many of the ghosts were more than 100 years older than he was. Yet, they were still ghosts. Steve was reminded of what that angel had told him. In the end, Steve found Halloween to be a nuisance. Why should he go racing around town with the other ghosts when he had much more important things to do in his own house.

Halloween came and Steve performed with the other ghosts. The next day there was no one in the house. This bothered Steve a little. There had been other times when everyone was gone for something called vacation. At night the Architect and Tom were home so it could not be vacation. Perhaps it was that other thing they called visiting Grandma. Tom had done that a few times and so had Alice.

A week passed and Alice finally came home. Alice had to stay in bed, though. This had happened more than once before. Steve did not mind. He could cheer Alice up anywhere. Steve did get the feeling the Nurse did not want him playing with Alice, but what mother would not want their child to laugh?

The Christmas season came. Steve could tell by looking out the windows and seeing all the decorations going up. Steve expected that the Nurse and Architect would start decorating any day. Steve had some special plans for the decorations that he thought would make this the best Christmas ever. Days went by and nothing happened. In fact, there was no Alice and no Nurse. Tom and the Architect slept in the house, but they were not around very often during the day.

Christmas was rapidly approaching. There were no decorations. There were no presents. Steve was angry. "How could they do this to me?" he thought.

A night came when no one was home. Steve decided he had to take matters in his own hands. Steve searched all over the house. He found the lights and ornaments for the tree, but he did not have a tree so he hung the ornaments all over the house. He found the nativity scene and he set it up just the way it was every year. Having a mother, a father, and a baby made him feel better, gave him hope. Finally Steve found the stockings. He hung them by the fireplace with great care.

Steve flew all around the house admiring his handiwork. "Not bad," he thought, "but I could have done much better if I had a tree."

Steve floated in his usual spot by the nativity scene. He missed the excitement of Christmas, all the songs, and all the joy. Steve was proud of the work he had done. He still missed the Christmas tree and all the presents. He remembered how much fun he always had watching everyone open the presents. At least he had hung the stockings even the one on which Alice had put his name. Steve had hung that stocking right in the middle because he thought it the most beautiful.

The sight of the empty stockings was too much for Steve. He flew up to his attic to get away. Steve tried to occupy himself by looking out over the town where he knew people were busy buying presents and enjoying Christmas with their loved ones. His thoughts kept on returning to the empty stockings. He had been so happy to receive Alice and Tom's presents last year. Now, Christmas was up to him and he had nothing to give. Was this what Alfred had meant when he said that the life of a ghost was hard?

Steve had not remembered Alfred's name until that moment. Steve had a thought, "Something terrible has happened to my family. I know it. I can't go out and search for them, but maybe I can go back to the gate to Heaven. Perhaps Alfred can help me." So Steve left his house and headed for the gateway to Heaven.

When Steve arrived at Heaven Alfred was still on duty. "Steve, back already are you?" Alfred asked him. If time passes quickly for a ghost it flies for an angel. All the time that had passed since Steve was last there had been only a few blinks of an eye for an angel.

Steve went right up to where Alfred sat behind his tall desk with his big book. "I've lost my family and I can't find them," Steve told Alfred.

Alfred was surprised by Steve's remark. "I don't understand, Steve. You are a ghost. How can you have a family?" said Alfred.

Steve answered, "Well, there's a mother and a father and a sister and a brother. They all live in my house. They are my family. Something is wrong and I don't know how to find them so I can help them."

Alfred thought for a while. He was about to tell Steve that there was no way he could help him when he saw the tears. Ghosts cannot cry. Oh, they boo-hoo and wail and moan, but real tears are not something a ghost can produce. Alfred knew that Steve producing real tears was something very special. "Steve," he said, "you have come a long way, haven't you? Let me see if I can help you."

Alfred started leafing through his big book. "Let me see," he said. "You are with the Architect and the Nurse, aren't you? Ah, here it is. Oh, my dear, this is bad news."

"What is it?" asked Steve.

"I am afraid that Alice is very sick. She is in the hospital," said Alfred.

Steve was hopeful. At least now he knew where his family was. "Is Alice going to get better?" Steve asked.

Alfred shook his head. "I am sorry, Steve," Alfred told him. "I cannot tell you that. What I can tell you is that Heaven is a very special place for children."

Steve took that to mean that something bad was going to happen to Alice. "It's not fair," he said. "Alice hasn't had a chance to live her life. Isn't there something I can do?"

Alfred looked at Steve. The defiant, bad person who had stood before him a short time ago was now this ghost crying over the fate of a little girl. The power of love, he thought, is the power of miracles. "Steve, I hesitate to mention this," he said. "There is something you can do. We have a long, technical name for it here in Heaven, but some of us just call it 'giving up the ghost.' I can't tell you what will happen. It could be very dangerous for you."

"You said 'giving.' I've been wanting to give something to somebody," Steve said. "How do I do it?"

"Go to Alice," said Alfred. "If this is what you truly want to do you will know how to do it, but, Steve, this may be too much to give."

Steve's mind was made up. "Nothing is too much for Alice," he told Alfred.

As Alfred watched Steve fly away he said two words

he never expected to say over a ghost, "Bless you."

9

The Search

Steve floated in the foyer staring at the front door.
Strictly speaking as a ghost Steve did not have to open the
front door to go through it. He was not worried about that.
Steve was trying to decide how to go about his search for
Alice. Did he try to ease into the outside world so he could get
used to feeling bad or should he just go at top speed and take
what comes? Steve decided that there just wasn't time enough
to take it slow. Steve went through the front door at top speed
and did not slow down until he was several blocks down the
road. At first Steve thought that he did not really feel that bad,
maybe this was not going to be a problem. Then it hit him full
force. A wave of weakness so strong that it knocked him to the
ground.

As Steve lay there he thought, "I should get back to my house. I guess a ghost just can't do something like this."

Luck would have it that Steve fell to the earth in front of one of those houses that people drive for miles to see at Christmas time. As Steve pulled himself up he saw the lights. It seemed as if every inch of the house was covered with lights. At the highest point was a star. The lawn had all sorts of decorations. There was a Santa Claus and reindeer, snowmen, carolers, and all sorts of animals. Most of all, right in the middle, was a nativity scene. Seeing the mother, the father, and the baby Steve was reminded of why he was there. "I've just got to do this," Steve thought.

Steve pressed on with renewed strength. He was going to need all the strength he had. That night was a particularly bad night to be out. It was windy and cold and a freezing rain fell that coated everything with ice. Ghosts, not having bodies, are not affected by the heat and cold the way we are, but they are affected. Steve, who had stayed inside his cozy house for so long, was especially affected. Still, Steve raced on to the center of town hoping to find the hospital and Alice.

The downtown area was all decorated for Christmas. There were angels or, as Steve thought, an Alfred on every streetlight. All the shops were decorated with lights. Every church had a nativity scene. The park in the center of town had a huge Christmas tree covered with lights. Steve took all this in as he searched the downtown area for the hospital. As much as Steve would have liked to stop and study everything he saw he could not stop until he found Alice.

Steve searched all over downtown. There was no hospital to be found. He was pretty sure that he was getting lost and searching the same area more than once because he kept on running into Santa Claus. At last Steve ducked into a little shelter. "I'm trying so hard," he thought. "I just have to find Alice before my strength runs out."

A voice boomed out of the dark. "What's your problem?' it asked.

Steve peered into the darkest corner of the shelter. "Why, you're a ghost," Steve said.

"So, what if I am?" the other ghost said. "You're a ghost, too."

"It's just I've never talked to another ghost, except, of course, at Halloween," said Steve.

The other ghost came out of the shadows and sat next to Steve. "You must be one of those lucky house ghosts," the other ghost said. "They never get out. I was a house ghost once and then they tore down my beautiful house and put up that park over there. Now I just wander around. If I go to far I start to feel sick. I spend most of my time watching over the park, but when the weather is real bad I duck in here."

"That's too bad," Steve said. "I never thought of myself as lucky. By the way, my name is Steve. Are there any other ghosts like you?"

"My name is Harold," the ghost said. "How do you do? There is a whole passel of ghosts without a home. Take a look around the town square."

Steve flew out of the shelter where he could take a good look. He saw about a dozen ghosts.

Steve returned to the shelter. "So many ghosts without a house to live in," Steve said, "I would never have guessed. What happened to them?"

"Over a century ago the downtown was a mixture of shops and homes," said Harold. "The city council got the idea to tear down all the old homes and put up offices and banks. When that happened they threw a lot of ghosts out into the cold."

"You sound like you don't like banks very much," said Steve.

"Oh, banks are terrible things," Harold said. "I know all about banks. I owned a couple. Now where is this house that you haunt?"

"I haunt the old mansion on the hill east of town," said Steve.

"I know it well," said Harold. "My cousin built it. He was always a strange sort, giving his money away all the time. He just would not listen to me. Now, answer the question. What is the problem that brings a house ghost so far from his house on a night like this?"

"I need to find the hospital," Steve told Harold. "I need to find Alice, the little girl that lives in my house. I've flown all around town and I can't find the hospital."

"That's because they tore down the old hospital and built a new one just north of town," said Harold.

"How do I get there?" asked Steve.

"The easiest way would be to follow one of those things," Harold said as a blocky vehicle in red and white with red and white flashing lights passed by. "I think they call it an ambulance. It takes sick people to the hospital. You'd better hurry and ask for Mabel when you get there."

Steve said, "Thank you," and took off after the ambulance. Steve chased it for miles and miles. He almost did not make it. Being away from his house was wearing him down. The only thing that kept Steve going was willpower. He just had to find Alice before it was too late.

The ambulance finally pulled up in front of a big building. People got out of the ambulance and transferred a person on a stretcher into the hospital. Steve followed them. Inside it was so noisy and bright with people everywhere. It was so different from his house. Steve tried to get away from all the noise and lights by going further into the hospital. Here Steve found the hospital to be not quite as bright and definitely not as noisy. Steve started to look for Alice.

Steve wandered around the hospital. There were hallways and doors everywhere. The hospital was so much more complicated than Steve's house. Steve had no idea where to start. Then he remembered what Harold told him. He should ask for Mabel.

Suddenly there was another ghost in front of him. She was holding a clipboard. "I'm Mabel. What do you want?" this new ghost asked.

"But you're a ghost," said Steve.

"What of it?" said Mabel. "I used to be a nurse here for over 40 years. This hospital would not run as efficiently as it does without me. I do not want any strange ghost causing any problems. Do you understand?"

"Yes, 'mam," said Steve.

"Good," said Mabel. "Now I have a lot of work to do and no time to waste. What is it you want?"

Steve found the idea of a ghost actually working to be a bit strange, but he had no time to waste either so he just asked, "How do I find a little girl called Alice?"

Mabel consulted her clipboard. "Yes, here she is," said Mabel. "There is a young girl named Alice in the Pediatric wing. Follow me and try to keep up."

Steve followed Mabel as she floated down a long hallway and up a few floors. Mabel stopped and turned to Steve. "This is the Pediatric wing," she said.

Steve did not even notice Mabel floating away because down the hallway he saw the Nurse and the Architect. They were talking to a lady in a long, white coat. Steve waited and watched. He saw the lady in the white coat shake her head. When the lady in the white coat left Steve saw the Architect and the Nurse embrace. Then they entered a room. Steve raced down to the room hoping he was not too late.

When Steve entered the room he saw Tom asleep in a chair. The Nurse and the Architect stood next to the bed, the Architect's arm around the Nurse and holding hands. There, in the bed, was Alice. Despite being hooked up to all sorts of strange devices Steve thought she looked as pretty as ever.

The Nurse looked up and then at the Architect. "Steve's here," she said.

"How can that be?" the Architect said. "Are you sure? I didn't think Steve could leave the house."

The Nurse just answered, "He's here. I can feel him."

Steve hovered over the bed. Alfred told him that if he really wanted to help Alice he would know what to do. Steve did not know what to do. He looked down at Alice. The thought of failing his friend was too much. His eyes filled with tears and one fell landing on Alice's forehead. A wind blew. Steve was gone.

Both the Nurse and the Architect saw the tear drop land on Alice's forehead. The Architect even scanned the ceiling to see where the leak was coming from. They both felt the wind blow The Nurse said, "Steve's gone."

Alice got better. The doctors all congratulated themselves. The new wonder drug, they said, had saved Alice's life. Her case was going to be presented and written up so everyone could know about the new wonder drug.

The Nurse and the Architect thanked all the doctors again and again, but the Nurse knew Steve was responsible for Alice's recovery. Even the Architect knew.

The first thing Steve noticed was that he was no longer a ghost. He was a person again. Then there was Alfred. He was no longer on his high chair, behind his high desk, but was walking directly toward him. Alfred came right up to him, took his hand, and put the other hand on his shoulder.

"Steve, I'm proud of you, my son," said Alfred. "You have earned your way into Heaven."

"Is Alice okay?" asked Steve. "She's not in Heaven, is she?"

"No, Alice is not in Heaven now," said Alfred, "but she will be many years from now and you will be here to greet her."

"Do I have to go to Heaven?" asked Steve. "I would really like to go back to Earth as a person. You see, I have a family now."

Alfred smiled. "I think we can work that out, Steve," Alfred said. "I just want you to know that we will be waiting for you when you are ready to come back."

10

Home

I stopped and stared into the dying fire. Erin sat curled up in a chair under a blanket. She had joined us about half way through the story. "Tom and Alice have been asleep for over an hour," she said. "You could have stopped telling the story after they fell asleep. Why didn't you?"

I cocked my head and looked at her. She had that wise smile she used when she thought she knew a secret.

"You could have stopped me. Why didn't you?" I asked.

"I saw you," she said. "You were staring into the fire. You definitely were in another time and place. Besides, it is a nice story. I enjoyed hearing it even if you don't know parts of the story to be true."

"What part of the story are you talking about?" I asked.

"Well, you could not have known that last part about Alfred," she said. "Why did you include it?"

I thought of telling Erin that the ending with Steve and Alfred made a better story, but I knew Erin would not be satisfied with that. I changed the subject. "It's almost Christmas. We ought to put Tom and Alice to bed. You carry Alice and I'll take Tom."

We headed upstairs. With the help of flashlights we put Tom and Alice to bed. We just took their shoes off and put them under the covers fully clothed. If the electricity did not turn on during the night we were going to have one cold Christmas in the morning.

Erin and I opted to get into bed with all our clothes on. I took one last look at my watch before switching off the flashlight.

"It's past midnight. Merry Christmas," I said to Erin.

"Merry Christmas, Randy," Erin said. "You never answered my question."

"What question would that be? There've been so many of them."

Erin poked me in the ribs. "You know very well what question, the one about Steve and the story you told. It's been two years since Alice was in the hospital and Steve, well, Steve left us. You've never mentioned Steve the whole time. I thought you didn't like Steve."

"I didn't. Tom and Alice and even my wife had an invisible friend. I was stuck cleaning up after a ghost. Some of it was frustration. I was also a little jealous. But tonight I sat there in front of the fire with Tom sitting next to me and with Alice on my lap and I couldn't help thinking how lucky we are. Sure, there's no electricity, but twenty years from now we'll talk about it like a great adventure. The main thing is that we've got each other and we are all healthy. So, there I was with Alice sitting on my lap, the greatest reminder of how lucky we are, and the story just came out. Getting Alice back was the best Christmas present I'll ever have. I know it is not rational, but I believe Steve was somehow responsible."

"I know," Erin said, "I believe that, too. When we came home from the hospital and I saw the house decorated with lights strung all over and Christmas decorations hung from everywhere it was all so bizarrely beautiful. Then I saw the stockings hanging by the fireplace with Steve's stocking, you know, the one Alice made for him, right in the middle I just lost it. I had to run to the bathroom so the kids did not see me cry."

"Yes," I told her, "I had a similar reaction. I put off taking down the decorations for weeks. I finally decided we had to move on, but I took photos just in case."

"You never told me about that."

"I didn't know whether we were mentioning Steve. Neither of us ever mentioned his name since that night in the hospital."

"Until tonight," said Erin. "When the kids asked about Christmas ghosts I guess I was hoping for this conversation. I miss Steve. When you are at work and the kids are in school I'll go up to the attic and sit in the rocking chair like I used to. When Steve was still here the attic seemed to be warm and friendly. Now it just seems empty."

"This was Steve's house, his home as much as ours," I said. "Like it or not, Steve was part of our family. Every night I lie awake in bed and hear a stray noise I find myself hoping Steve has come back. I didn't add the last part of the story with Alfred the Angel. It just came out. I guess that is what I am hoping for. That Steve will come back to us. If Alice was the best present ever then getting Steve back would be a close second."

We were quiet for a while. There was a knocking at the front door. "Who could that be at this hour," I said. There was more knocking, louder this time.

"Better go down and see who it is," said Erin. "It must be one of the neighbors that need help."

I got out of bed, put my shoes on, and headed down the stairs. When I opened the front door there was no one there. I stepped outside and searched the front porch with the flashlight. I found two big bags of gaily wrapped presents. I walked to one end of the porch and then the other. No one was there. I heard a sound coming from the direction of the street. I went down the few steps of the front porch. My flash picked up a man in the middle of the front yard. Before I could say anything he yelled, "Merry Christmas, Randy. Come on out. It is only a little snow." I went back in and grabbed a coat before joining the stranger in the middle of my lawn.

As I approached I kept the flash trained on the stranger. When I got close enough I could see it was a young man. I was about to ask who he was when he held a finger up to his lips. "Listen," he said. The snow was coming down steadily, but not heavily. There was not even the touch of a breeze. If you listened carefully there was a fine hiss. "Hear that?" he said. "That is the sound ghosts make when flying."

I thought that a rather odd comparison. I started to ask again, but the stranger broke in. "I missed last Christmas so I brought extra presents. I hope you don't mind. I'm not very good at buying presents yet, but I think I have the perfect one for you. It is something that no one knows you've wanted for years."

Again, it was rather strange to have someone I could not recognize tell me they had the perfect present for me. Before I could say anything he went on. "I have so many questions. Is Alice all right? Is she as pretty as ever? And Tom, does he still have that spirit of adventure? He was always so much fun. And Erin, she always wanted three children. You two are such great parents. You should have a third child."

I was surprised to hear someone I did not know talk about my family that way. This time I beat him to the punch. "Who are you?" I asked.

The stranger smiled and stuck out his hand. "Oh, I am sorry," he said. "I thought you knew who I was. My name is Steve."

It took a second or possibly two to get over my shock.

After all, it was like seeing a ghost. I threw my arms around

him and said, "Welcome home."

www.ingramcontent.com/pod-product-compliance
Lightning Source LLC
Chambersburg PA
CBHW071411170626
46811CB00003B/1353